KITTY CORNER

DUCHESS

ELLEN
MILES

SCHOLASTIC INC.

New York   Toronto   London   Auckland

Sydney   Mexico City   New Delhi   Hong Kong

*With special thanks to my
kitty expert Kristin Earhart,
for all her help.
This book is dedicated to Catherine,
who loves cats.*

ISBN 978-0-545-27574-3

Cover art by Mary Ann Lasher
Cover design by Tim Hall

12 11 10 9 8 7 6 5 4 3 2 1   11 12 13 14 15 16/0

Printed in the U.S.A.   40

First printing, November 2011

CHAPTER ONE

"What are you drawing?"

Mia Battelli looked up to see Logan staring down at her sketch. His long brown bangs hid his eyes.

"It's the traffic circle by the park." Mia brushed eraser bits off the paper. Her class was studying maps, and everyone was drawing part of the neighborhood around the school. When they were done, they were going to build a miniature version of their neighborhood out of clay, showing the school, the park, their houses, and other important places. Their teacher, Ms. Rivera, called it a diorama.

"Why did you draw a cat on that building?" Logan asked. He jabbed a finger at Mia's sketch.

Mia didn't like the way he pointed at her drawing. What was Logan Barrow doing at her desk, anyway? He usually sat on the other side of the room. "That's Wags and Whiskers," Mia said. "The cat is there to show it's the veterinary office."

"Ms. Rivera said we're only supposed to include important places." Logan twirled his pencil between his thumb and two fingers.

"Wags and Whiskers *is* important," Mia said. "We take all our foster cats there." The Battelli family had fostered two cats—actually they were both kittens—so far. Mia and Michael and their parents had taken care of the kittens until they found forever homes for them. Mia had told her class all about it at meeting time.

"Well, it's okay for your sketch. But Ms. Rivera has to approve it for the diorama." He twirled his pencil again.

Mia scowled. "You're right. It's up to Ms. Rivera," she said. Mia happened to know that Ms. Rivera had a cat *and* a dog. Their teacher would definitely agree that the vet's office was important enough to be on their map.

Why was Logan bugging her? He hardly ever talked to her, probably because they had nothing in common. Everybody knew that Mia loved cats. Logan, on the other hand, loved sharks. He wore his shark T-shirt nearly every day, and he had already done about three oral reports on sharks that year. He spouted shark facts the way other boys spouted baseball statistics. Mia was not interested in sharks—or Logan.

Logan shrugged. He started to turn away, then stopped. "I know a cat you could foster," he said.

Mia blinked. "You do?"

"Yeah." Logan looked right at Mia. "Our neighbors are moving, and they can't take their cat with them. She's really fancy. All poofy and white."

Now Logan had Mia's full attention. "Is she a Persian?" she asked. She pictured an elegant cat with long white hair, bright round eyes, and a flat, wide face.

3

"Yeah, I think so," Logan said. "Do you want her?"

Did Mia want to foster a Persian? She always wanted to foster new kitties, and her family had never fostered a purebred cat before. It sounded too good to be true. She squinted at Logan. "Why don't you take her?"

"We can't," Logan answered. "My dad's allergic to cats. And dogs. And horses. Just about everything."

"Logan, Mia?" Ms. Rivera called from her desk. "Is there something you want to share with the class?"

Logan stood up straight. "Just going to sharpen my pencil," he said.

"The sharpener is up here, not at Mia's desk," Ms. Rivera reminded him.

Over at the next table, Nicole Strauss nudged Merry Winters, and they started to whisper and giggle. Mia rolled her eyes. Why did certain

4

people have to make a big deal about it whenever a boy talked to a girl?

"Oh, yeah," Logan said. He headed toward the front of the room. Nicole and Merry giggled some more, until Ms. Rivera shot them a look.

Mia felt her cheeks burn. She bent her head and concentrated on her drawing. She wanted to ask Logan more about the Persian. What was her name? How old was she? When could they pick her up? But Mia knew she had to talk to her parents first. Fostering a cat was always a family decision—a big one.

When the last bell rang, Mia rushed to her cubby and grabbed her backpack. She glanced around for Logan. He was walking toward the door with a bunch of friends.

"Hey, Logan!" she called. Logan looked over his shoulder. "What about the cat?" she asked.

Logan shrugged. "I'll talk to my mom and call you later," he said as he headed out the door.

Mia frowned. So much for getting some answers.

She headed for the stairs, where she usually met Michael. Her brother was in fifth grade. He was tall and skinny for his age, and he had big feet, so she could always hear him bounding down the steps before she could see him. "Ready?" he asked when he appeared.

"Ready," Mia said. Michael had promised to walk around the neighborhood with her so she could get more ideas for her map.

"Guess what?" she asked Michael as they left school. "We might have another cat to foster." She told Michael what Logan had said about the Persian cat. "I want to talk to Mom about it, but I don't even know the cat's name yet."

"I wouldn't tell Mom or Dad until you know the details," Michael said. "Don't get your hopes up."

Mia sighed. Michael was right. How could she convince Mom to foster a cat she didn't know anything about? It was better to wait until Logan called with more information.

They hiked up and down every street in the neighborhood. Mia took notes and drew little pictures to help her remember landmarks. After a while, Mia's stomach began to growl. She remembered that Mom had given them money for a snack at Mrs. Lopez's bakery. Mia sniffed the air as they walked. She knew they were getting closer to the bakery when a sweet smell drifted through the air. "What are you going to get?" she asked.

"A black-and-white cookie," Michael answered, just as she'd known he would.

Mia ducked under his arm while he held the door open. "You always get that," she said. Mia could never decide. She looked at the shelves of pies and colorfully decorated cakes and at the glass cookie jars on the counter. "Maybe I'll get a lemon bar today, since we'll probably order cupcakes for my party next week." The Battellis had been on vacation for Mia's last birthday, so now, six months later, her parents had said she could have a half-birthday party.

7

"Maybe Mrs. Lopez could decorate them with cat faces," Michael suggested.

"Oh, that would be so cool," Mia said. Her brother knew how much she loved cats of every kind. Siamese cats, tabby cats, calico cats. Fat old cats and tiny kittens. Wild cats, like tigers and lions. She loved them all. Mia was definitely going to ask Mom if she could have kitty cupcakes.

When they had gotten their treats, they walked out of the bakery and down the street. Mia took little bites to make her lemon bar last longer.

The Battellis lived in a brownstone building around the corner from the bakery. When Mia and Michael turned onto their street, Mia spotted Mom outside with her watering can and pruning shears. Mrs. Battelli worked at a nearby garden shop, and their house was full of plants—inside and out.

Mom straightened up from a prickly rosemary bush. "Hey, guys," she called as she shielded her eyes from the sun.

8

"Hi, Mom." When Mia hugged her around the waist, she could smell the spicy scent of rosemary. It reminded her of spaghetti and meatballs.

"Anything exciting happen today?" Mom asked.

"Nope," Michael said as he loped up the stairs and went inside.

"How about you, Mia?" Mom said.

Mia thought again about the Persian cat but remembered what Michael had said. She was dying to tell Mom, but it was probably better to wait until she knew more. "Not really," she replied.

"Hmm," said Mom with a funny little smile. "Well, I'd say that promising to foster a new cat sounds pretty exciting to me."

CHAPTER TWO

"What?" Mia stared at her mother. She gulped. How had Mom found out? "I didn't promise anything. This boy in my class, Logan, told me about a cat. He was supposed to find out more and call me. I don't even know her name."

"Duchess," Mom said. "Or should I say '*the* duchess'? That's what Logan's mom called her." She pulled off her gloves, shook out the dirt, and tucked them into the pocket of her gardening apron. "Will you get the watering can for me?" she asked as she headed inside.

Mia grabbed the can. Mom didn't sound mad, but she didn't exactly sound happy, either. "Why did Mrs. Barrow call you?" Mia yelled as she hurried down the entry hall after Mom. "Logan was supposed to call me." Mia kicked off her shoes and followed Mom into the kitchen. "I was waiting to get more information before I told you—I mean, asked you—about fostering her," Mia explained. She felt frustrated. Why couldn't Logan have called her first, the way he'd said he would? Now everything was all messed up.

"It's true," Michael said to Mom. "I told her to wait until we knew more." Michael grabbed an apple and brushed by Mia on his way out of the long, narrow kitchen. "I think fostering an adult cat sounds like fun," he called over his shoulder.

Mia wished he hadn't left them alone. She could use her brother's help right now.

Mom sighed and tucked her hair behind her ears. "I'm not upset with you," she said. "It was just a big surprise. Logan's mom said her neighbor really needs someone to take the cat before she moves." She frowned. "I called Dad at work to talk about it already, but I hate to rush things. Fostering a cat is a big decision."

11

Mia nodded. "I know," she said. "That's why I wanted to make sure Logan was being serious."

"I think he was," Mom said with a laugh. She reached out and squeezed Mia's hand. "It's okay, Mia. Logan's mom is going to tell Duchess's owner, Abby, to email us," Mom told her. "Until we hear from her, how about if you start your homework?"

Mia realized that there was no point in begging Mom to foster Duchess until they knew more about her. She didn't really have any homework that day—she'd finished her math problems during class—but she had an idea about something else she could study. She grabbed the family laptop and joined Michael at the dining room table.

"What are you doing?" Michael asked as she opened the computer.

"I'm going to read about Persian cats," she said. "I want to be prepared." Mom and Dad expected Mia and Michael to help as much as possible with their foster cats. Mia loved petting them and playing with them and making sure they had enough to eat and drink. She was even happy to help clean out the litter box! She wanted to prove that she and Michael were ready for a cat of their own.

There was plenty of information online about Persian cats. It didn't take Mia long to learn that they were the most popular breed in the United States. She read that Persians were the perfect "lap cat," since they were loyal pets who enjoyed attention. She also read that because of their long coats, Persians needed more brushing than most cats. That wasn't a big deal. Mia would take turns with Michael, and if he didn't want to brush Duchess, she'd do it all by herself.

"Have you seen the laptop?" Mom walked into the room. "Oh, you have it," she said to Mia. "Are you done with your homework?"

Mia nodded. "I was reading about Persian cats," she said. She smiled up at Mom. "Just in case."

"That's a good idea," Mom said. "But let's not get ahead of ourselves." Mia scooted the laptop so it was in front of Mom's usual chair. Maybe Duchess's owner had already sent Mom an email! Mom sat down and began to type.

Mia pulled a library book out of her bag, but she couldn't concentrate on the story. She kept thinking about Duchess. She glanced at Mom. Had she checked her email yet?

"Well, here it is," Mom said.

"What? The message from Duchess's owner?" Mia hopped up and went over to Mom. She leaned over her shoulder until her face was right along-side Mom's.

"Mia, please give me some space," Mom said.

Mia straightened up. "What does it say?" she asked.

"Let's see. Abby says that Duchess is a four-year-old Persian, and she's great with kids. Here's a picture." Mom clicked twice, and a color photo popped up on the screen.

Mia gasped. "She's beautiful!" Duchess was just as pretty as Mia had imagined she would be. Her long white hair, her round, flat face, her fluffy tail . . . She looked just like the Persians Mia had seen online.

"She is lovely," Mom admitted. "Look at those gorgeous blue eyes."

Michael glanced over at the laptop screen and made a face. "Is she wearing jewelry?"

"It's her collar," Mia said. A sparkly heart pendant hung from Duchess's neck. "It's pretty."

"If you say so." Michael shrugged.

Mom went back to reading the message. "They're moving out of the country, to Iceland, where Abby's husband grew up. Duchess would have to be quarantined, and they don't want to put her through that."

"What's 'quarantined'?" Mia asked.

"Some countries require pets to stay in a kennel for weeks and weeks, to make sure they don't have any diseases," Mom explained. "Abby says

15

Duchess has never spent a night away from home in her whole life. It sounds as if they really need to find Duchess a home right away—like today!"

"Oh," said Mia. She could understand why Abby thought it would be better for Duchess to find another home.

Mom looked at Mia. "I suppose it would be a good experience for you and Michael to foster an adult cat."

Mia knew what that meant. Mom had decided, even without talking to Dad again. They were taking Duchess. "Yes! Yes! Yes!" She jumped up and danced around. "When can we get her?"

"Abby says here that we can pick her up any-time—the sooner, the better," Mom said as she closed the laptop and pushed back her chair. "Who wants to come?"

CHAPTER THREE

Mia held Mom's hand and skipped to their car, which was parked on the next block. They were going to get Duchess! Michael didn't seem as excited about the fluffy white cat, and he had lots of homework to do. Nonna Kate, their upstairs neighbor, had come downstairs to stay with him.

Mia loved to spend time with Nonna Kate, but she wasn't about to miss out on picking up Duchess—not for the whole world.

"I'll bet she's super sweet," Mia said as she fastened her seat belt in the backseat. "I can't wait to pet her. She looks so soft."

"I know you're excited, sweetheart." Mom looked at her in the rearview mirror. "Just remember to take it easy."

Mia nodded. She knew that some cats needed time to warm up to new people.

Mia watched out the window as they drove. It wasn't long before Mom parked on a tree-lined street. "This is it," Mom said. She pointed to a brick town house with window boxes full of color-ful flowers.

Mia looked around. She wondered where Logan lived. She was still mad that he hadn't called her. He had almost ruined everything.

They climbed the stairs, and Mom rang the bell. As they waited at the front door, Mia peeked in the window. She saw stacks of cardboard boxes, rolled-up rugs, and piles of books waiting to be packed. But she did not see a fluffy white cat. Finally, a woman with short red hair and blue-framed glasses came to the door. "You must be Julia and Mia," she said. "I'm Abby. Come on in."

"It looks like you're moving soon," Mom said.

"In two days," Abby said with a sigh. "If I ever finish packing, that is! I'm not making

18

much progress with these guys getting into everything."

Mia looked down and saw two toddlers crawling between the boxes. They looked exactly alike, both with the same red hair as their mother. "They're twins!" she said.

"They sure are," Abby said with a smile. "Lola and Jake. They can crawl faster than I can run." Mia watched Lola climb over Jake to pull herself up on a box full of books. "Not now, peanut." Abby knelt down and swooped a child onto each hip. "Sorry," she said. "You didn't come here to meet my kids. You came to meet my lady. I think she's in the bedroom, on her chair."

Mia held her breath as she followed Abby and Mom through the kitchen toward the back of the apartment. "There you are!" Abby sang. "Hello, Duchess. You have visitors, little lady."

There on a blue and white chair sat the prettiest cat Mia had ever seen. Her long white hair shone, her blue eyes sparkled, and her fluffy tail moved slowly from side to side. She looked like a queen, sitting regally on her throne. She glanced up at Abby and blinked.

That's me! I'm the only one she talks to that way. I'm her sweet little lady.

Mia sighed. The cat was even more beautiful in real life than she had been in her photo. Mia wanted to rush up and pet her. No, she wanted to pick her up and bury her face in all that silky fur. But she knew she had to be patient. She didn't want to frighten Duchess.

Abby put Lola and Jake down, and the twins toddled back toward the kitchen. Abby knelt next to Duchess. She stroked the thick white fur around the cat's face. "Oh, Duchess. I'm going to miss you, lady." Mia could hear a deep, rumbly purr from across the room. Duchess closed her eyes and rubbed her face along Abby's hands.

20

She knows where to pet me. I showed her how when I was just a kitten. She learned well.

Abby gazed lovingly at Duchess. Mia wondered if she was going to change her mind.

Then a loud clatter erupted from the kitchen. Abby shot up and ran toward the sound. "Oh, no! I think they've gotten into the fridge!"

Mia looked down at Duchess and noticed that the cat's ears were laid back instead of pointed up. That usually meant that a cat was upset or frightened. Duchess stood up on her chair and looked toward the kitchen. "It's okay, Duchess," Mia said. "It's just Lola and Jake, getting into something. Abby will take care of it."

Duchess licked her lips and then settled down on her chair.

"Can I pet her now?" Mia asked Mom.

"I think that would be fine," Mom said.

Duchess's long white fur was even softer than Mia had expected, but the cat did not seem as relaxed as she had been when Abby was petting her. Mia noticed the way a furry ear flicked back each time she ran her hand along Duchess's back.

"Oh, good," Abby said as she came back to the room. "I'm glad you're getting acquainted. Duchess is great with kids. And Sally Barrow said you've fostered cats before," said Abby, looking at Mom.

"Yes, we think it's a good way for the kids to learn about the responsibility of having a pet before we get one of our own," Mom explained.

"Well, maybe Duchess will be the one you keep," Abby said. Mia felt a flutter of hope. Fostering cats was great, but she really wanted one of her own someday.

"Maybe," Mom said. "But one way or another, we'll find the best home for her. You can count on that."

"That's wonderful," Abby said. There was another loud noise from the kitchen. She sighed and looked over her shoulder. "What are they up to now?" She rushed out again.

"Maybe?" Mia looked at Mom. "Did you say 'maybe,' as in maybe we'll keep Duchess forever?"

Mom rolled her eyes. "Don't push it, Mia. We're fostering her, and that's plenty for now. Let's get her home. It's almost dinnertime."

"Maybe you're the one," Mia whispered excitedly to Duchess. She tried to pet her under the chin the way Abby had, but the cat jumped down from the chair and walked away.

"She knows something is up," Mom said.

Mia nodded. She had read about how pets often seemed to sense when their owners were going on a trip or when visitors were coming to the house.

Abby appeared again. This time, she was holding a cat carrier. "I didn't realize how late it has gotten," she said. "Jake and Lola need to eat, so I guess I'm going to have to send you an email with all the instructions for taking care of Duchess. It's not too complicated, but there are some things to remember. For example, you have to take special care of that beautiful coat of hers. She likes to look her best. Don't you, my lady?" Abby laughed as she gently coaxed Duchess into the carrier. Then she held a treat up to one of the circular airholes. A pink nose poked out, and the treat was gone.

"And here are her toys, her blanket, and some other things." Abby handed a bag to Mia.

She gave the carrier to Mom. "Julia, thanks so, so much," Abby said. "It's hard to say good-bye, but it's easier now that I know she'll be in good hands." Mia noticed that Abby was talking more quickly now. "Please keep in touch and let me know how she is."

Jake and Lola crawled out from behind a desk. "There you two are!" Abby said as she swooped down to lift them up. "Now, it's time to say good-bye to Duchess, guys," she said. Her voice cracked.

She led Mia and Mom to the front door. "So long, Duchess," Abby whispered. "Say bye-bye," she told Lola and Jake. She gazed at the carrier as she squeezed her twins tightly, and Mia could see that she had tears in her eyes.

Mia felt a lump in her own throat. "Bye-bye," she said, waving at the twins.

Mia saw Duchess's round face looking out the back of the carrier as they walked down the stairs. The pretty Persian let out one long, low meow, and Mia felt the lump in her throat grow bigger. Poor kitty! "Don't worry," she said, touching the top of the carrier. "We'll take good care of you, Duchess."

CHAPTER FOUR

"She's a lot heavier than Callie was," Mom said as she lugged the carrier up the stairs of their brownstone building.

"She's a full-grown cat," Mia said. "Aren't you, Duchess?" Mia could see the cat's pretty face through the grate at one end of the big plastic carrier. Her velvety ears were pinned back. "We're almost there," Mia reassured her.

Mom handed Mia the keys so she could unlock the front door. "We're back!" she called down the hall.

Nonna Kate popped her head out of the apartment door. "We've been waiting," she said.

"Nonna Kate's been waiting," Michael said when Mom and Mia walked inside. "I was doing math."

"Good for you," Mom said.

"Oh, just look at her!" exclaimed Nonna Kate. She bent down to get a closer look. "She is a duchess, isn't she? Absolute royalty." When Nonna Kate held out her hand, Duchess gave it a long sniff.

Very good. This person knows royalty when she sees it. And I like her kind voice.

Mom placed the carrier on the floor in the middle of the family room.

"Can I let her out?" Mia asked. "It's cramped in there. The grate is like a cage."

"It's no place for a duchess," Nonna Kate agreed.

"You may release the prisoner," Mom said with a laugh.

Mia loosened the latch, swung open the door, and waited. "Come here, Duchess. Here, kitty," she cooed. But Duchess didn't budge. Her ears were still back as she twitched her tail against the carrier wall.

27

Where am I? Where is my person? I don't want to be here. It doesn't smell like home. It isn't *my home.*

"Why isn't she coming out?"

Michael knelt down next to Mia and looked into the carrier. "She doesn't look very happy to be here."

"Well, she hasn't given us a chance," Mia said, frowning. "She doesn't even know where she is."

"Yes," Nonna Kate said slowly, "but she knows where she isn't."

Mia looked at their upstairs neighbor. That made a lot of sense.

Nonna Kate stood up. "Well, I'm going to head upstairs. I'm hosting a card game tonight." She leaned over and tapped a nail on Duchess's carrier. "You take care of this lady, now."

"Can't I just pull her out?" Mia asked when Nonna Kate had left.

"No, I think we should let her come out on her own," Mom said. "The crate may seem small, but it helps her feel safe. It's important that she decides when she's ready to come out. It's getting late. Let's order pizza. Mia, you can help me make a salad and we can talk about your half-birthday party." Mia remembered that she and Mom had planned to work on invitations that day.

"How many kids do I get to invite?" Mia asked as she and Mom began to pull lettuce, tomatoes, and cucumbers out of the fridge.

Mom thought about it for a moment. "Does ten sound like a good number?"

Now Mia took a moment to think. In her mind, she counted up the people she wanted to invite. Carmen, the twins, Wilson, Nikkya, Audrey, Leo, Yuki, Annie, and Annie's little sister (to be nice). Then she nodded. "Ten is perfect," she said. "And I want to have kitty invitations and kitty cupcakes."

Mom smiled. "Of course you do," she said.

A little later, as Mia tossed a handful of raisins into the big wooden salad bowl, she heard the front door open. "Dad's home!" she yelled. She ran into the hallway to greet him.

29

"Daddy, we got a new foster cat!"

"I heard, I heard," Dad said. "I guess you're happy about that."

"Not just happy," Mia said. "I'm—I'm"—she remembered a word Ms. Rivera had used in class the other day—"elated! You've got to see her. She's beautiful."

"Okay, Miss Elated Mia May. Just let me put my bag down first."

When he'd dropped his bag and keys, Mia led Dad over to the carrier.

"You haven't let her out yet?" he asked.

"No, she hasn't *come* out yet," Mia corrected him. "We're letting her take her time."

"Look at that collar!" Dad said. He whistled. "Pretty fancy!"

"Nonna Kate says she looks like royalty," Mia said.

"She acts like it, too," Michael said. "She thinks she's too good for us commoners."

"That's not true," Mia said.

The doorbell rang. "That's the pizza!" Mom called from the kitchen.

"I'll get it," Dad called back, pulling out his wallet.

Mia and her family sat down to eat—the pizza was Mia's favorite, a pie with onions and extra cheese—but Mia couldn't concentrate on dinner. Mom frowned at her. "Mia, I'm going to ask you to change seats if you can't stop staring at the cat," she said.

Mia looked up. "There's something wrong," she said. "Duchess hasn't meowed. Not even once."

"Maybe that's a good thing," Dad suggested. "Remember Otis? His meow was more than we could handle."

Mia smiled. Otis, the last cat they had fostered, had a habit of yowling all night. Nobody had gotten much sleep during the time they'd had Otis—except for Mia, who could sleep through anything.

"Honey, maybe Duchess is just a little sad,"

Mom said. "It's natural. She's going to miss Abby and her old home for a while."

Mia sighed. "Maybe we need to know more about how to take care of her. Wasn't Abby going to send us an email with more information? Can you write to her?"

"I think Abby has enough going on right now. Maybe you could call your friend Logan. They're neighbors, right? He probably knows a little about Duchess."

"Logan's not my friend," said Mia. She was still mad at him for not calling her when he'd said he would.

Later, as Mia helped clear the table, she looked over at Duchess. The cat was sleeping—not on the comfy pillow Abby had given them, but inside the carrier. Duchess was curled up in a white ball, her nose tucked neatly under her fluffy tail. With her eyes closed, she looked peaceful. Mia wanted her to be that happy when she was awake. But what would make Duchess happy?

Mia had no idea. Any bit of information would help, wouldn't it? "Okay, I'll call Logan," she said, as she brought the last dirty dishes into the kitchen.

"Just keep it short," said Dad. "It's almost bedtime."

"I'll be quick," Mia said. It wouldn't take long. How much could Logan really tell her? After all, Duchess was a cat, not a shark.

Mia found her class list and dialed Logan's number. When he answered the phone, Mia suddenly felt nervous. Maybe it would be better to talk to his mom. But she took a deep breath and jumped in. "Hi, Logan. It's Mia Battelli. We picked up Duchess today."

"You did?"

"Yeah, after your mom talked to my mom." Mia bit her lip, remembering again how mad she'd been at Logan. But that wasn't why she'd called. That wasn't important anymore, now that they had Duchess. "Thanks for telling us about her."

33

"No problem. I told my mom you'd take really good care of her."

"Um, thanks," Mia said. "Well, I don't know if you can help, but I'm calling because we didn't get to talk to Abby very long, and we want to know more about Duchess. You know, what she likes and stuff like that."

"Hmm, I don't know that much about her," Logan said.

Mia rolled her eyes. This call was a waste of time. Why ask a shark boy when you needed cat facts?

But then Logan went on. "I mean, Abby got Duchess as a present about four years ago. I remember because it was right when my little brother was born. Abby used to bring Duchess over to our house all the time for visits. Duchess usually just slept in her lap. But whenever Abby brought her windup mouse, Duchess would pounce on it over and over. She never got tired. My little brother thought it was hilarious. And Abby used to sit with Duchess on the porch and brush her for hours. Seriously." Logan paused. "But I haven't seen Duchess much since the twins were born."

Mia scribbled down just what Logan said, but she had a hard time keeping up. He might not think it was much, but to Mia this was treasured information.

"I don't know if that helps."

"I think it will," Mia said, and she meant it.

"Mia, honey." Dad tapped his watch. "Bedtime."

"I'm sorry, Logan," she said. "I better go."

"Okay. See you tomorrow, Mia."

Mia said good-bye and hung up. Logan had actually been kind of nice!

Mom walked into the kitchen. "Maybe you should invite Logan to your party."

"Um, maybe," Mia said. She headed to the bathroom to brush her teeth. What was Mom thinking? He might have been nice this one time, but it wasn't as if she and Logan Barrow were friends.

CHAPTER FIVE

The next morning, on her way through the living room, Mia checked the carrier. It was empty! Duchess had finally come out. But where had she gone? Mia held her breath as she knocked on Michael's door. "Is the cat in there?" Mia asked, her fingers crossed.

"Nope."

Phew! Mia was glad Duchess had come out of the carrier, but she would *not* have been glad if Duchess had slept with Michael, who didn't even care about her that much. But if Duchess wasn't in the carrier and she wasn't in Michael's room, where was she?

That was when Mia got a whiff of breakfast. Bacon. As soon as she stepped foot in the kitchen doorway, she saw Duchess. The white cat sat on the wooden floor in a patch of sun. She practically glowed in the morning light as she sniffed the air and licked her chops.

Mom looked up and smiled. "Look who's hungry," she said. It took Mia a second to realize that Mom meant Duchess. "She didn't touch her food from last night, but I'll bet she eats this morning."

Duchess had her chin up and her ears pricked forward. Her nose quivered as she smelled the bacon. Mia slowly walked up to her, reached out a hand, and scratched behind her ear. Duchess ducked her head and walked away.

Why is she petting me now? Can't she see I'm hungry?

"Can I feed her?" Mia asked.

"Sure, her food's in the fridge," Mom said. "I found a couple of tins in the bag with her other stuff after you went to bed."

Mia frowned. Their other foster cats hadn't eaten canned food. They had both loved Kitty Nibbles, which came in a big yellow bag. Oh, well. Every cat was different. That was part of the fun of fostering. She got a can from the fridge and grabbed a spoon. "Here, Duchess," she said as she plopped a heaping spoonful of Savory Salmon Stew into a bowl. Duchess didn't move. Mia tapped the spoon against the bowl the way she'd seen people do on commercials. "Yummy salmon for you," she sang. "Doesn't it smell delicious?" Actually, Mia thought it was the stinkiest stuff she'd ever smelled, but she knew cats liked fish.

Duchess glared at Mia with ice-blue eyes and flicked her silky tail back and forth.

Cat food. Ha! I don't want cat food. I want what the woman is cooking. I'm sure she's making it for me.

"It's time for breakfast. Just leave her food by the water bowl and wash up, Mia." Mom patted the bacon with a paper towel and put it on a platter. "Dad had to leave early, so all this bacon is just for us."

"Yum," said Mia. She loved bacon.

Duchess followed Mom to the table, walking right past her savory salmon. Mia frowned.

Duchess sat next to Mom's chair and stared up at her. "Your food is in the kitchen, Duchess," Mom said as she ate a bite of oatmeal. She smiled at Michael, who had just joined them, then turned back to shake her head at Mia. "And, Mia, remember you can't play with Duchess while you're at the table. It's time to eat."

Mia sighed and slumped down in her seat as she nibbled a piece of bacon. Mom always came up with lots of rules when they had a foster cat. Mia looked at the kitty, who was winding herself elegantly around Mom's legs. Even if she couldn't play with Duchess, she could talk about her. "Want to hear what Logan said about Duchess?" Mia asked. She told Mom and Michael everything she had learned.

"So she's used to lots of attention," Michael said.

Mia nodded. "At least she used to be. But remember while we were there, Mom? Abby was always leaving to check on the twins."

"So maybe Abby's been too busy lately," Mom said.

Mia nodded. Then she saw Duchess jump up into Dad's empty chair. Surprised, Mia stared at the cat. Uh-oh. Mom wasn't going to like that! Slowly, the white cat put her front paws on the table. Her long white whiskers twitched as she sniffed the air with her pink nose.

Oh, that smells so good. Where is mine? I'm so hungry, and they aren't sharing. That's not very nice.

"Oh, no you don't." Mom waved her hand at Duchess, who quickly jumped to the floor. "That's right. Go eat your own food," Mom said.

"She might be royalty, but she has horrible manners," Michael said. Duchess walked straight into the kitchen, her tail whipping back and forth.

Mom looked as if she wanted to giggle as she watched Duchess sashay away. Then her face got serious again. "No cats at the table," she said.

Another rule, thought Mia. Wouldn't it be better to spend their time figuring out how to make Duchess happy, instead of making up rule after rule?

That day at school, Mia spent a lot of time daydreaming about Duchess and thinking about what Logan had told her. By the time she met Michael by the stairs, she was sure she had figured out what to do to make Duchess feel at home.

"We have to brush her," Mia said as soon as she saw her brother. "She loves it. Plus it's super important to keep her long fur from getting knots in it."

"I was thinking that, too," Michael said.

Mia looked at him doubtfully.

"I was!" he said. "Didn't Logan tell you that Abby made a big deal out of brushing her all the time?"

"Right," Mia said. "So we should make a big deal out of it, too."

As soon as they got home, Mia found three brushes and two combs in Duchess's bag. Next she found Duchess in the dining room, sprawled out on Dad's chair. "Sorry, girl," Mia said as she scratched Duchess under the chin, "you're not allowed on there." Mom was working in the back-yard. If she saw Duchess at the table again, she would not be happy. Gently, Mia lifted Duchess off the chair. She sat down on the rug next to the pile of brushes and pulled Duchess onto her lap, but Duchess quickly stood up and started to walk away.

"She's too big for my lap," Mia complained to Michael, who had just come in from the kitchen.

"Don't give up so easily." Michael picked Duchess up and sat down next to Mia. "Now, I'll hold her and you brush."

Mia looked at the three brushes and chose a pink one with rubber bristles. "You'll like this, Duchess," Mia promised. Duchess looked at the brush, blinked her eyes, and relaxed in Michael's lap. As Mia started running the brush along her back, Duchess craned her neck around to smell Mia's hand.

It's been so long since I've had a good brushing. I have to admit it feels wonderful, even when this commoner does it.

"I'm going to do your tummy," Mia said, but as soon as she started to brush the longer hair on Duchess's belly, the brush stopped on a tangled clump. Mia gave it a tug, but the brush was stuck. The cat's ears went back.

Duchess hissed, stood up, and walked away with the brush still hanging from the matted hair on her tummy. Then she stopped and bit at the brush.

Mia frowned. "That wasn't supposed to happen."

"We can't just leave it there," Michael said.

Mia hurried after the cat. "Wait, Duchess, I'll help you. It won't hurt, I promise." Duchess stood still as Mia carefully reached under her belly, using one hand to hold the hair and the other to loosen the brush until it came out. "There," Mia said. Duchess quickly sat down and started licking the spot where the brush had been tangled.

Thank goodness she got that thing off me. I love to be brushed, but I hate when it hurts. I don't really trust kids—like those little ones who took up all of my person's attention. But I suppose this girl is doing her best.

Duchess looked at Mia and blinked her blue eyes. Then she leaned forward and licked Mia's hand with her rough pink tongue.

Mia was flattered. Finally! Maybe Duchess was starting to like her. "Her tongue's like sandpaper," she said with a giggle. Duchess strutted away and jumped right back onto Dad's chair.

Mia sighed. "Oh, Duchess. What are we going to do with you?"

CHAPTER SIX

"Why does she always ignore us? All we want to do is play with her." Mia took a bite of vegetable lasagna and looked around the dinner table.

The Battellis were having a family chat. They were trying to figure out what to do with Duchess. She had been with them for four days, but she still hadn't warmed up much. That afternoon, Mia and Michael had tried to get Duchess to play. She wouldn't chase a string, a catnip ball, or even the special windup mouse that Logan had said she'd liked. "She didn't even pounce on it once. She just sat on her pillow and looked at us like we were crazy," Michael said as he ripped off a piece of bread and popped it into his mouth.

Mia looked at Duchess, a big white fur ball with

a rose-petal-pink nose, still curled up on her bed.
Mia nodded. "The mouse ran right into her, but she acted like she didn't care. She just lifted up her paw and cleaned her whiskers."

"She's *always* primping like that," Michael said.

Dad snorted. "Maybe she's getting ready for the royal ball."

"I don't get it," Mia complained. "Abby said that she's good with kids, but she usually just walks out of the room whenever me and Michael come in."

"She's never mean, but she's not exactly nice, either," Michael said.

"Maybe that's what Abby meant by being good with kids," Mom suggested. "Maybe Duchess pretty much ignored the twins, and that was a good thing."

"Yeah, they probably didn't really want to play with her," Mia said. "But we do."

"I'd say the biggest problem is that she still isn't eating," Dad said. "I'd sure be in a bad mood if I hadn't eaten in four days."

47

"Mia and I were worried about that, too," Mom said. "We emailed Abby to see if she had any suggestions, and she wrote back with some ideas. Unfortunately, it sounds like Duchess has some bad eating habits." She told Dad and Michael that Abby had admitted she had often fed Duchess people food, even though the vet had told her that it wasn't good for cats. Duchess was a picky eater and hardly ever ate her own food without something special mixed in. Abby would make Duchess grilled chicken breast or fresh fish and feed her in the dining room, right along with the family. "Chicken Kiev was her favorite," Mom finished, laughing. "But she won't be getting that from me. I have a hard enough time making dinner for the four of us. I'm not making a gourmet meal for a cat, too."

Out of the corner of her eye, Mia could see Duchess waking up. She opened her mouth wide and uncurled her tongue from between her white teeth. Duchess stood up and shook her fluffy

48

white mane. Then she hopped off her cushion and trotted over to the table.

"Oh, I see we're awake," Mom said. Duchess stared up at her with unblinking eyes.

It's dinnertime! I hope they'll share something with me this time. I'm so hungry.

"She always wakes up at dinnertime," Michael noted. "It's about the only time she pays attention to us."

"Now, Michael, let's not be too hard on the poor cat," Mom said. "Mia, do you want to get Duchess's dinner ready?"

"Sure," Mia said as she scooted back her seat.

"Did you make her chicken Kiev?" Dad asked.

"Very funny," Mom said, smiling at Dad.

"I'll help Mia." Michael got up and joined Mia in the kitchen. "So what are we going to feed her?" he asked.

"You heard Mom," she said. "Duchess is picky,

but we're not giving her people food." Mia mixed some wet and dry food together as she talked. "But Mom doesn't want to risk Duchess getting sick. So Abby suggested mixing all the cat food up, putting treats on top, and crossing our fingers that she likes it."

"You can bring the bowl in here," Mom called. "Maybe she'll eat it on the floor."

"Where'd we get that crystal bowl?" Dad asked when he saw Mia walk in with Duchess's dinner. This time Mia had put the food into a special glass dish that turned different colors when it caught the light.

"It was in Duchess's bag. I hadn't noticed it until Abby told me to look for it. It was all bundled up in bubble wrap so it wouldn't break," Mom explained.

"Abby said it was Duchess's special bowl, so maybe she'll want to eat out of it," said Mia. "Here, Duchess. This is for you."

The Persian looked up when she heard her

name. As soon as she saw the bowl, she curled herself around Mia's legs. Duchess gave the bowl a quick sniff and started to eat. Mia could hear a low, rumbling purr as the cat dug in. Mia gave Duchess a quick pet before going back to her seat. She was happy to see Duchess eating. Finally!

"Well, now that we've got her eating, let's move on to the next problem," Mom said. "I'm sure we all agree that Duchess would be happier somewhere else."

Mia swallowed hard. That wasn't exactly true. She still dreamed about keeping Duchess forever.

"Maybe Duchess would like having another cat around," Mom went on. "It might perk her up a little. My friend Catherine from work has a cute little kitten named Boone, and she's looking for an older cat to keep him company. I'd like to tell her about Duchess. Is everyone okay with that?" Mom looked around the table, her gaze resting finally on Mia. "Just think how happy Duchess would be if we found her the right home."

Mia looked at the fluffy white cat. Duchess was busy licking the last bits of food from her dish. She licked the tip of her nose, and then she lifted her paw to comb back her whiskers. Mia did want her to be happy and loved. That was the most important thing. "Okay," Mia said.

"I'll call Catherine tonight. If she's interested in giving Duchess a try, we might even be able to take her over there tomorrow." Mom put her napkin on the table and announced that there was mint chocolate chip ice cream for dessert.

When Mom got up, Duchess walked over to Mia's chair and rubbed her face against Mia's ankle. Mia sighed. The pretty Persian was finally starting to warm up, just when she might be leaving. Mia understood that they needed to find her a home, but the next day seemed too soon. She looked down at the fluffy white cat. She knew Duchess wasn't exactly the adorable, playful kitten she'd always wanted, but it still wasn't easy to say good-bye.

CHAPTER SEVEN

When Mia woke up, the sun was shining through her window. She smiled as she sat up and stretched. She loved sleeping late on Saturdays! Then she remembered that Duchess might be leaving that day, and her heart sank. She still didn't even know Duchess very well. How could she be sure Catherine was a good match for her?

Mia took off her pajamas and pulled on her favorite blue cords and a cozy red sweater. She headed straight for Duchess's pillow and used both hands to scratch the white cat behind her ears. Duchess lazily lifted her chin and looked at Mia.

That feels nice. I do enjoy a good ear rub. This girl is catching on.

Duchess seemed almost as if she was enjoying the petting, for once. But then, a few moments later, the regal white cat stood up, twitched an ear, and walked out of the room.

Mia sighed. Then she went into the kitchen, pulled down a box of cereal, and fixed herself a bowl for breakfast.

"You're up and dressed early today," Mom said as she came into the kitchen, holding her gardening gloves. She plucked a raisin out of Mia's cereal bowl and popped it into her mouth.

Mia nodded. "I need to learn everything I can about Duchess before she goes."

"You're taking this much better than I thought you would." Mom rubbed Mia's shoulder. "I spoke to Catherine last night after you went to bed. She said she'd like to meet Duchess this afternoon."

Mia took a deep breath. "We need to meet Catherine, too. We might not be the right family for Duchess, but I still need to make sure that she is."

"So you'll come with me?" Mom asked.

"I wouldn't let you go without me." Mia smiled up at her.

Mom smiled back and ruffled Mia's hair. "I'm glad you're serious about finding the best match. We'll go after lunch," she said as she opened the door to the backyard. "Don't forget that Catherine has a kitten."

Mia's heart sped up at the very thought of seeing a kitten, but she needed to focus on Duchess. Dad had taken Michael to his basketball practice, so Mia was on her own that morning.

"Okay, girl," Mia said as she reached under the cat's belly to lift her. "I'm going to brush you. You need to look pretty for Catherine." Mia sat down and crossed her legs. "Let's try this again." Duchess let out a small meow as Mia set her on her lap.

Careful, now. Be gentle, and don't get that brush stuck again!

Just as Mia was about to start, she heard a light knock on the door.

"Yoo-hoo! It's Nonna Kate. I wanted to check on the duchess."

Mia let Nonna Kate in and sat back down with Duchess. "I'm brushing her so she looks good for her new home," Mia explained.

"Is that so?" Nonna Kate settled in to watch. Mia tried to hold Duchess with one hand and brush with the other, but Duchess did not make the job easy. She squirmed around, trying to bite the brush.

"May I show you something?" Nonna Kate asked.

Mia looked up and nodded.

Nonna Kate moved over to sit next to Mia. She looked through the brushes and combs Mia had laid out and picked up a metal comb. "My cat Murray was a Maine coon, so I know all about long hair. If you start with a comb, it helps get out the tangled parts. With this beautiful long coat, Duchess needs a good brushing every couple of days." As she spoke, Mia's neighbor gently moved the comb through the soft hair on Duchess's tummy. "See? She has many layers of hair down here. The comb removes the dead hair so it doesn't get ratty." Nonna Kate scratched Duchess under the chin. "You're a pretty pussycat, not a little rat." With a rumbly purr, Duchess rolled over and held her paws up in the air so Nonna Kate could really reach her belly.

This is more like it. I deserve some real pampering.

Mia was amazed. "She loves it when you brush her."

"I enjoy it, too. You'd better like brushing if you have a Persian. Persians are a lot of work," Nonna Kate said.

"We're learning that," Mia admitted.

"But you're worth it, aren't you?" Nonna Kate said to Duchess.

Mia hoped Catherine would agree.

After lunch, Mia packed up Duchess's brushes and her pillow. She rinsed out her crystal dish and put the canned and dry cat food and the kitty treats in a big plastic bag. The drive over to Catherine's was quick.

"Thanks for coming, guys," Catherine said when she opened the door. "You, too, Duchess." Catherine brushed her wispy blond bangs from her eyes as she leaned over to peek into the carrier. "What a sparkly collar you have."

"Where's Boone?" Mia asked, looking around for the kitten.

"He's in the bathroom," Catherine said, motioning to a nearby door. "When you introduce two cats, it's best to do it slowly so they can get used to each other. We wouldn't want them to start off with a fight."

"Oh, I don't think Duchess would ever fight. She's a lady," Mia said.

"You never know," said Catherine. She led them into a bedroom with lots of sunlight and a wall of bookshelves. "This is the guest room. I thought Duchess could stay in here until she and Boone are comfortable with each other."

Mia wasn't sure that Duchess would like being stuck in one room. Duchess was the type of cat who liked to roam around and find the most comfortable places to perch.

"I'll spend plenty of time with her so she has lots of love, and, in a couple of days, she and Boone can meet face-to-face," Catherine explained. "I hope they'll become best buds. Boone really needs a playmate."

Catherine bent down and opened the carrier. "Let's give her a chance to come out of the carrier on her own time. Why don't we go meet Boone? Be sure to close the door behind you."

Mia was torn. She hated to leave Duchess

alone, but she was dying to see the kitten. "I'll be right back," she promised Duchess. As soon as Mia left the room, she saw a tiny kitten bounding past the bathroom door. Her heart melted. Boone was white with gray splotches all over, even on his tail. His bright green eyes looked mischievous. He batted at a yellow plastic ball, and it rolled under a dresser.

"I'll get it, Boone," Mia said as she reached under the dresser. When she pulled out the ball, Boone's eyes grew brighter. She threw the ball, and he scampered after it. *Click, click, clack!* His tiny claws clattered against the wood floors as he skidded to a stop. Mia laughed out loud.

"Boone's a little clown," Catherine said with a smile. "He's got gobs of energy. I hope another cat will mellow him out."

Mia nodded. She wondered if Duchess was the right cat for the job. Just then, Boone trotted up to his dog-sized water bowl and walked right in.

"Oh, my gosh! He's in the water," Mia said. Water sloshed over the side of the bowl as Boone leapt out.

"Yep, that's my boy," Catherine said.

Mom and Catherine talked while Mia played with Boone. Mia threw him a catnip mouse over and over again. Then he chased her shoelaces and tried to eat them. Mia overheard Mom telling Catherine all the details they'd learned about feeding Duchess and about Duchess's special crystal dish. Mia chimed in with Nonna Kate's advice about grooming Duchess every other day, starting with the metal comb. Finally, Mom stood up and said they had to get home.

Mia grabbed her coat off a chair. "I just have to say good-bye to Duchess." But when Mia opened the door to Duchess's room, that quick little Boone slipped in before she could stop him. The curious kitten ran right up to the carrier, stuck his head inside, and took a sniff.

"No, Boone!" Mia grabbed the kitten just

as Duchess swiped a paw at his face. "It's okay, Duchess. He's just a kitten." But when Mia looked in the carrier, Duchess hissed at her.

"Hmmm," said a voice behind Mia.

Mia turned to see Catherine standing in the doorway with her arms crossed and a frown on her face. Uh-oh. Maybe Duchess wasn't the perfect pal for a pesky kitten like Boone after all.

CHAPTER EIGHT

Mia felt terrible the whole way home. She hadn't meant to let Boone into the guest room. She had ruined Catherine's plan for slowly introducing the two cats. And she hadn't even had the chance to say a nice good-bye to Duchess. After Catherine had taken Boone out of the room, Duchess hid in the back of her carrier. She swatted her tail back and forth and ignored Mia.

"I tried so hard to be friends with her," Mia said.

"You did a good job," Mom assured her. "Duchess is just a hard nut to crack."

Mia looked at Mom. "A hard nut?" she repeated.

"It just means that it isn't easy to tell what she's thinking." Mom tapped her finger on the steering wheel. "Don't feel bad, Mia. Do you know what I'm thinking?"

Mia shook her head.

"I'm thinking it's a good thing Duchess will be out of our house for your party next Saturday. I don't think she would have liked all the kids there, or all of the attention."

Mia thought about that. Mom was probably right. But was Duchess really going to learn to get along with Boone? Catherine had agreed to give it a chance, but Mia was not so sure things were going to work out. Duchess still might be back at their house next week on the day of the party.

The party! With Duchess around, Mia hadn't had much time to think about her party. She and Mom had mailed the invitations last week, and people were starting to call to say if they could come. Mia hadn't heard from Wilson yet, and Audrey had said she couldn't come because she had to go to her grandmother's.

Mom kept bugging Mia to invite Logan, but so far she hadn't. Mia was pretty sure he'd say no if she did invite him. They hadn't talked since their phone call, so Mia was surprised when he came up to her desk on Monday morning at school.

"How's Duchess?" he asked.

"We might have found her a home," Mia said.

Logan smiled. "That's great."

"I hope so. I just want her to be happy," Mia said.

"Sure," Logan agreed. "She's a good cat, even if she isn't super playful or cuddly with people she doesn't know."

Mia was impressed that Logan understood Duchess so well.

"Anyway, thanks for taking her," he said. "It's great that you get to foster cats. I wish I could help sharks somehow. But really, I only started liking sharks 'cause my dad's allergic to everything else."

Mia laughed. "You sure do know an awful lot about them, Logan."

Logan rolled his eyes. "But I won't be fostering one anytime soon. I should get to my desk." He motioned to the clock and started to turn away.

"Hey, Logan," Mia said. "Want to come to my birthday party? It's my half birthday, actually. Anyway, it's on Saturday, at two o'clock."

Logan looked surprised. Mia couldn't blame him. She'd surprised even herself with the invitation. "I don't know," he said. "I've got a soccer game that day."

Mia swallowed. "Oh, that's okay. My brother always has games on Saturdays, too."

Mia watched Logan walk away. Now she felt kind of sorry that he wouldn't be able to come to her party. But with or without Logan, the party was going to be fun. She was going to have cat cupcakes—what could be better than that?

When Mom came home from work that night, she had news from Catherine. Duchess was still on her own in the bedroom. She seemed fine, except that she hadn't been eating.

On Tuesday night, Mom had more news. Catherine had let Duchess out of the bedroom for an hour. She reported that Duchess and Boone were slowly getting used to each other.

Mom had Wednesday off, so there was no update from Catherine. That night, Mom and Mia put together the favor bags for her party and talked about games. Mom had some great ideas, and Mia came up with a few, too. The games would be silly, but in a good way, and Mia thought her friends would love them. They all fit the cat theme, like Pin the Tail on the Puma and a hide-and-seek game with chocolate mice.

At dinner on Thursday, Mom told everyone that Catherine was ready to let Duchess out of the bedroom for good. "It sounds like she's finally settling in," Mom said hopefully. "Catherine has tomorrow off, and she's going to spend a lot of time making sure Duchess and Boone get to know each other."

But on Friday afternoon, the telephone rang. Mom and Dad were still at work, and Nonna Kate was watching Mia and Michael. All three of them were busy playing Monopoly on the rug, so they let the answering machine get it. Mia recognized Catherine's voice right away.

"Hi, Julia, it's Catherine. Could you give me a call? It's about Duchess, and it's important. Thanks. Bye."

"We should call Mom on her cell," Michael said.

Nonna Kate put her hand on his shoulder. "Let's not worry her. Your mom will be home any minute," she said.

"But what if Duchess is hurt?" Mia asked. "What if she and Boone got into a fight after all?"

Nonna Kate smiled at her. "That Duchess is a strong, smart cat. Don't you worry. She can take care of herself."

*   *   *

Mom called Catherine as soon as she got home. She looked at Mia, Michael, and Nonna Kate as she hung up. "Catherine asked us to come over later tonight."

"Did Duchess get in a big fight with Boone?" Mia asked.

"I don't think so," said Mom. "But I'm not sure they're best buddies, either. I guess we'll find out more tonight."

After dinner, Mom and Mia put on their coats and drove over to Catherine's. Mia held her breath as she rang the doorbell. When Catherine opened the door, Mia was surprised to see that she was smiling.

"Is Duchess okay?" Mia asked.

"She's fine," Catherine said. "But I asked you to come over because I think we have a problem."

"What problem?" Mom asked.

"Well," said Catherine. "The problem is that

Duchess doesn't seem to be such a good fit here. I wanted her and Boone to be friends, but I'm not sure that's ever going to happen. Boone gets in her food and knocks over her fancy dish. He leaps in her water bowl and splashes her when she tries to drink." Catherine shook her head. "Duchess doesn't like it. She's never hurt him, but she's always batting him away. I'm worried that she might scratch or bite him."

Mia didn't want Boone to get hurt, but she had to hide a smile. Nonna Kate was right. Duchess *could* take care of herself.

"And with all the brushing and the special food, she's more work than I can handle." Catherine took a deep breath as she poured tea into three cups. "I asked my friend Annette for advice since she has lots of experience with Persians. In fact, she has three of them. And . . . well, it turns out that Annette might be interested in Duchess! She'd love to come over and meet the cat — and you — if you think it's okay."

Mia swallowed. Three cats? She looked at Mom.

"I can see you need to think about it," said Catherine. "Let's sit and have a cup of tea while we talk. Mia, Duchess is in the guest room if you'd like to say hi. I thought it might be best to keep her and Boone separate for now."

Mia went down the hall to the guest bedroom. She wondered where Boone was. It would be fun to play with him again. But right now, she needed to see Duchess. Somehow she knew that the pretty Persian needed her.

Mia opened the guest room door and peeked in. The white cat was curled up in her crate with the door open. Mia slipped inside the room, careful this time to make sure Boone wasn't trying to get in, too. "Hey, Duchess." Mia knelt down and held out her hand. Duchess blinked and yawned as she sniffed Mia's outstretched fingers.

The girl is back. It's good to see her. At least she isn't always in my face like that little kitten.

71

As Mia gently scratched Duchess behind the ear, she thought about Annette and her three cats. It was obvious that Duchess wasn't a good match for Catherine and Boone, but would Annette's family be right for her? Wouldn't it be hard for Duchess to get the special attention she needed in such a crowded house? It wasn't fair to bounce Duchess from home to home.

Mia took a deep breath. Suddenly, she knew there was something important she had to say. She had to speak up. Duchess's happiness depended on it. She went back into the living room where Mom and Catherine were still talking. She waited until there was an empty moment in the conversation. "Um," she said. She took another deep breath. "I think maybe Duchess should come home with us. I think we need to find Duchess a home where she is the only cat."

Mom raised an eyebrow, then smiled at Mia. She nodded slowly. "You know, honey, I think you're right."

Catherine smiled and nodded, too. "I think Duchess is lucky to have such a good friend who understands what she needs. My friend will be disappointed, but Annette loves cats, just like you do. She'd want whatever is best for Duchess."

Once again, Mom and Mia loaded Duchess's carrier into the van and drove home.

"I'm proud of you for speaking up, Mia," Mom said as she turned down their street. "But now we have another problem."

"What do you mean?" Mia asked.

"What are we going to do with Duchess during your party tomorrow? She won't like all those kids running around and yelling." Mom glanced at Mia in the rearview mirror.

"I've got that all figured out," Mia said. "We just have to ask a favor."

"A favor? From whom?" Mom asked.

"From someone who loves and understands cats," Mia said.

73

CHAPTER NINE

Mia ducked under pink and purple party streamers as she carried Duchess up the stairs to the second floor of their brownstone building the next morning. Michael was right behind her with Duchess's pillow and comb and a day's worth of food piled in his arms.

"Nonna Kate!" Mia called as she knocked on the wooden door. "We're here." Duchess mewed and fidgeted in Mia's arms.

What's going on? Is she going to drop me? I don't really fit in this girl's little arms.

"Hold on, Duchess," Mia said soothingly. "You'll have a good time today with Nonna Kate. It'll be quiet and you won't have to run away from all the kids downstairs."

"You're lucky, Duchess," Michael said. "I wish I could hide from a houseful of third graders, too."

Mia scowled at her brother just as Nonna Kate opened the door.

"Well, hello," Nonna Kate said. She smiled at the cat in Mia's arms.

"Hi, Nonna Kate. Thanks so much for taking care of Duchess today."

"Anytime, really," said Nonna Kate. "We have a big day planned, don't we, Duchess?" She took Duchess from Mia and began to pet her. Mia saw Nonna Kate's long, glossy nails run through the fluffy hair under Duchess's chin, and she heard Duchess purr in contentment. Duchess stretched out one paw and squeezed her eyes shut happily.

Now that's nice. This person knows how to hold me. And she knows how to give a good scratch, too. Nice, soft, and slow.

"Thanks, Nonna Kate," Michael said as he dropped Duchess's stuff by the sofa. "We'll come and get her after the party." Then he turned to Mia. "Come on. We still have lots to do!"

Mia waved and hurried down the stairs. Her friends would be there any minute!

It wasn't long before the party was in full swing and the backyard was filled with music and laughter. Mia had just taken her turn at hitting the giant lion piñata when Michael called her inside. "You have another guest," he said, tilting his head toward the front hallway.

Mia looked curiously at the kitchen clock. She thought all her friends were already there. Whoever had just arrived was really late!

Then she saw Mom talking to someone in the front hall. "Mia!" Mom called. "Logan is here. I was just talking to Mrs. Barrow. Come say hi."

Logan? That was a surprise. When she stepped into the hall, she saw Logan standing there, still in his soccer uniform, shin guards and all. "Hey," she said.

"Hey. Sorry I'm late," Logan said. "My game ended early, so we came straight from the park. I knew from your map at school that it was close." He smiled and thrust a present toward her. The wrapping paper was covered with soccer balls. "Here. Sorry it's not cat wrapping paper. They didn't have any at the store."

"Thanks," Mia said. She smiled at him. Logan was okay. "Guess what?" she asked. "We had to take Duchess back from my mom's friend. That didn't work out so well. Her kitten was too much for Duchess. Now we're looking for someone who wants only one cat so she can get tons of attention. Do you want to see her? She's right upstairs, with our neighbor."

"Sure," said Logan.

Mia led Logan up the stairs. She knocked lightly on Nonna Kate's door. "Nonna Kate? Are you there?"

"Come on in," Nonna Kate called. "The door's open, sweetheart."

Mia cracked the door open and saw her neighbor sitting on the couch with Duchess sprawled out by her side.

"Nonna Kate, this is Logan. He's the one who told us about Duchess. He wanted to see her."

"Hi," Logan said with a nod. "It's nice to meet you."

"Nice to meet you, too." Nonna Kate looked down at Duchess. The Persian leaned into Nonna Kate's hand, lifting her chin a little to show Nonna Kate just where to scratch.

A nice, easy afternoon on the couch. I hope I can stay here. It sounds noisy downstairs, and I really would like to take a nap.

Mia thought Duchess seemed more relaxed than she had ever seen her. Every once in a while, Duchess's ear would flick back at the sound of an excited scream from the backyard, but she seemed happy on the couch.

Logan knelt down to let Duchess smell his hand. "Hey, Duchess, I hope you find a good home," he said.

"Oh, she will," Nonna Kate assured him. "She's a lovely cat and she'd be a good friend and companion. Anyone would be lucky to have her."

"Hey, Mia!" Michael called from downstairs. "It's time for cupcakes!"

Mia smiled at the thought of the frosted kitties on the chocolate cupcakes they'd bought for the party. She had her eye on a white cat with bright blue eyes, and she couldn't wait to blow the candle out and make a wish. She smiled at Duchess, who was purring loudly as Nonna Kate softly stroked her silky fur. This year, Mia had a feeling she could make her wish come true.

CHAPTER TEN

Mia loved having cupcakes for her birthday—especially cat cupcakes! Mom put one pink candle in the middle of Mia's, right on top of the cat's nose. As Mia blew out the flame, she crossed her fingers and made her wish.

The cupcakes from Mrs. Lopez's bakery were delicious. Everybody loved them—except Michael, who was eating a black-and-white cookie instead. Mia had asked Mom to order one just for him.

After cake, Mia opened her presents. Carmen gave her a cool rain forest poster with a jaguar playing in the river. It made Mia think of Boone jumping in his water bowl. Wilson, her friend from art class at the rec center, gave her a jewelry-making kit. She got lots of games, a DVD, and some cute rain boots. But Mia's favorite present came from Logan. He gave her two books: *500 Cool Cat Facts* and *500 Stunning Shark Facts*.

"My mom told me to give you something I'd like to get," Logan said.

Mia flipped through the shark book, looking at all the amazing photos. "I'll still never know as much about sharks as you do," Mia said.

"Probably not," Logan said. "And I'll never know as much about cats as you do."

Mia smiled. She wasn't so sure of that. He already knew a lot about Duchess.

When the party was over, Mia plopped down on the sofa between Mom and Dad and played with the string of a balloon. She was exhausted.

"Whew! Finally, it's quiet in here. I'll go get Duchess," Michael said, heading for the hallway door.

"Wait," Mia said. "Before you do that, I want to have a family chat."

"Right now?" Mom asked.

"Right now," Mia said. "It's important."

Michael sat down in the rocking chair.

"Well, what is it?" asked Dad.

Mia wound the balloon string around her finger. "It's about Duchess," she began. "We still need a good home for her, right?" Mia looked around. Mom, Dad, and Michael all nodded. "And we think she'd rather have a home without kids. Right?" They nodded again. "And since she didn't really get along with Boone, we think she probably needs a family where she's the only cat. Right?"

Mom and Dad were still nodding, but Michael was starting to look impatient.

"I'm almost done," she promised. "When Logan and I went upstairs to see Duchess, she was sitting on the couch with Nonna Kate. She seemed really happy. She was even purring. And Nonna Kate looked pretty happy, too." Mia paused. "What if we asked Nonna Kate if she wants to adopt Duchess?"

Mom sat up and looked at Mia. "Mia, that's brilliant!" she said.

Michael raised his eyebrows.

"I don't know why we didn't think of it before," Dad said. "Sounds like a great idea to me."

"Yeah," Michael agreed. "Remember when Catherine called and we were all worried about Duchess? Nonna Kate said that Duchess was strong and could look out for herself. It's like she understands her better than anyone."

"There's just one catch," Mom said. "We don't know if Nonna Kate wants a cat."

"She'll want Duchess," Mia said. "I'm sure of it. But let's go ask her right now." She stood up. "Who's coming with me?"

Michael stood up. "I am."

"And me," Dad said.

"I don't want to be left out," Mom said. "But let's be sure Nonna Kate doesn't feel like she *has* to take Duchess."

With that, the Battellis marched up the stairs and knocked on their neighbor's door.

"Come on in. It's open," Nonna Kate said. Her eyes grew wide when the whole family trooped in. "Goodness. Surely it won't take all four of you to carry this little treasure down the stairs." She reached down to pet Duchess's back as the cat nibbled food out of her crystal dish. Mia could hear Duchess's rhythmic purr from across the room. Then she realized that Duchess had not walked away when she and Michael had come in, the way she often had before. *She really must be comfortable and happy here with Nonna Kate*, Mia thought.

Mia realized that Nonna Kate was staring at her with a curious look on her face. She felt Mom nudge her from behind. She took a deep breath as she thought of what to say. "Nonna Kate? We're so glad you watched Duchess today."

"Nonsense. It was no problem. We got on like two peas in a pod, didn't we, Duchess?" The cat sat up. Her food bowl was empty. Nonna Kate reached down and lifted Duchess into her lap. Duchess began to purr even louder.

Oh, a nice cuddle. I deserve that. I am such a good girl.

Mia turned around to look at Mom, who smiled encouragingly. "We're wondering if you would like to keep Duchess a little longer," she finished. "Like maybe for good."

Nonna Kate raised her eyebrows. "Me?" she asked. "Keep Duchess?"

Now Mia looked at Michael. He nodded at her to keep going. "It's just that Duchess seems so happy with you. You'd give her lots of love, and she could keep you company." Mia paused again. "You could be Duchess's forever family, if you want."

Nonna Kate's face broke into a grin. "I want, I want!" Nonna Kate exclaimed. "I have so enjoyed

Duchess today. I forgot how nice it is to have a cat around, and Duchess is such a dear." She stroked the furry white cat from head to tail while Duchess purred. "Are you sure you all don't want to keep her?" the older woman asked.

"We want the best home for Duchess," Mom said, "and we think it's with you."

"Oh, thank you," Nonna Kate said. "I will happily be Duchess's forever family." She quickly looked up. "But how was the party?"

"Super fun," Mia said.

"Good. I liked your friend Logan," Nonna Kate said.

Mia smiled. "He's okay for a boy who likes sharks." Maybe Logan really was her friend after all.

Michael stepped forward. "We brought you this." He placed a kitty cupcake on the table in front of their neighbor.

"Oh!" Nonna Kate laughed out loud. "It looks just like you, Duchess. A gorgeous new cat and a yummy cupcake. It feels like *my* birthday," she said. Duchess purred even louder.

Mia smiled. Duchess and Nonna Kate were so happy together. Her birthday wish had come true.

KITTY CORNER CAT QUIZ

True or False?

1. **All cats are independent. They groom themselves and do not need help from people.**

2. **Cats sometimes swallow their own fur.**

3. **Brushing your cat is hard work.**

Read on for the answers.

**1. All cats are independent.
They groom themselves and
do not need help from people.**

FALSE. It's true that some cats are very independent. But all cats need help with grooming from time to time. Just how much help depends on the cat. Persians (like Duchess) and other long-haired breeds require daily brushing. Long hair is more likely to develop mats, or messy knots, that a cat cannot untangle on her own. Mats can be painful and can eventually hurt a cat's skin. Cats need to be brushed often to keep their coats healthy. Short-haired breeds need brushing, too, but only every one to two weeks.

**2. Cats sometimes swallow their
own fur.**

TRUE. All cats swallow some hair when they clean themselves. After all, their sandpapery tongues are designed to remove loose hair!

Sometimes, if a cat swallows too much fur, she will cough up a hair ball. Yuck! This is disgusting, but normal. If it happens a lot or seems to upset your cat, take her to the vet.

3. Brushing your cat is hard work.

FALSE. Brushing your cat is easy! Ask at a pet store which brush or comb is best for your cat's coat. When brushing, remember to stay calm. Your cat will know if you are tense, and she will get nervous, too. Brush her for only a couple of minutes the first time. Figure out where your cat likes and doesn't like to be brushed. Always finish with the spot your cat likes best. Then give her a treat, pet, or play with her so she looks forward to getting groomed again.